SPOOKY SLEUTHS

The Ghost Tree

SPOOKY SLEUTHS

Read them all . . . if you dare.

SPOOKY SLEUTHS 1

The Ghost Tree

Natasha Deen

illustrated by Lissy Marlin

A STEPPING STONE BOOK™

Random House 🏠 New York

Text copyright © 2022 by Natasha Deen
Cover art and interior illustrations copyright © 2022 by Lissy Marlin

All rights reserved. Published in the United States by Random House Children's Books, a division of Penguin Random House LLC, New York.

Random House and the colophon are registered trademarks and A Stepping Stone Book and the colophon are trademarks of Penguin Random House LLC.

Visit us on the Web!
rhcbooks.com

Educators and librarians, for a variety of teaching tools, visit us at
RHTeachersLibrarians.com

Library of Congress Cataloging-in-Publication Data
Names: Deen, Natasha, author. | Marlin, Lissy, illustrator.
Title: The ghost tree / Natasha Deen; illustrated by Lissy Marlin.
Description: New York: Random House Children's Books, 2022. |
Series: Spooky sleuths; 1 | "A Stepping Stone book." | Audience: Ages 6–9. |
Summary: "When Asim moves to a new town, he must save his new teacher when an evil spirit from Guyanese folklore begins to wreak havoc."—Provided by publisher.
Identifiers: LCCN 2022003757 (print) | LCCN 2022003758 (ebook) |
ISBN 978-0-593-48887-4 (trade) | ISBN 978-0-593-48888-1 (lib. bdg.) |
ISBN 978-0-593-48889-8 (ebook)
Subjects: CYAC: Supernatural—Fiction. | Spirit possession—Fiction. |
Folklore—Guyana—Fiction. | Guyanese Americans—Fiction. | LCGFT: Novels.
Classification: LCC PZ7.1.D446 Gh 2022 (print) | LCC PZ7.1.D446 (ebook) |
DDC [Fic]—dc23

Printed in the United States of America
10 9 8 7 6 5 4 3 2 1

This book has been officially leveled by using
the F&P Text Level Gradient™ Leveling System.

For my grandparents —N.D.

*To my family. Thank you for
your support. —L.M.*

1

Mom came downstairs as Dad and I were eating breakfast.

"Asim, it's your first day," she said. "Do you want me to walk you to school?"

"I'm good," I said. Two days ago, we'd moved to Lion's Gate, Washington, for my parents' jobs. Mom was a marine biologist, and Dad was an astrophysicist. They were excited to work for Eden Lab because it was the best research facility in the world. The lab handled secret projects, too. That's why Lion's Gate was the only town on the island. It was also the creepiest town. *Ever.* Strange lights in the forest, hovering objects in the night sky.

"If we walk together," Mom said, "we could take a peek at the cemetery."

Mom and I loved spooky stuff. She was always telling me tales from when she grew up in Guyana. We loved supernatural creatures so much that we had a bunch of notebooks full of stories we'd collected. At least, Mom thought they were stories, but I knew supernatural creatures existed. So I wasn't going to

mess around in a cemetery—there could be ghosts! "Still good," I said.

"We don't want you to get lost," said Dad, wiping crumbs from his red beard. "You're our favorite son."

I groaned at his dad joke. "I'm your only son," I said.

After breakfast, I zipped the house key in my bag and headed out.

Our house was on top of a hill. Below it was the town. The day was cold, windy, and foggy, but I could see the cemetery.

Even with the clouds, the graveyard cast its shadow. The wind picked up and tickled the back of my neck with icy fingers.

I shivered and pulled my jacket close. As I walked down the hill, I heard voices. Through the mist, I saw some kids. I waved.

They waved back but kept walking.

I hurried to catch up. Even if they didn't talk to me, at least I wasn't going to be alone walking past the cemetery. At the bottom of the hill, they turned left toward school. I sped up, turned, and saw another creepy thing about this town.

The abandoned houses.

My hands grew cold at the sight of

overgrown grass and dead trees. The shutters groaned on rusted hinges. The broken windows were soulless eyes staring into me. My heart thumped. I tore my gaze away from the gaping doors and looked for the kids.

They had disappeared into the mist.

"That's impossible!" I said to the empty street. But I was alone, staring at the cemetery on the other side of the road. Gloomy shapes spread from the black iron gates and oozed along the cobblestone paths. Weeds reached out from between the posts and tangled together on the sidewalk.

"Don't be afraid," I whispered, and crossed the street. The weeds pushed along the pavement. They twisted like wriggling snakes, waiting for me to get closer before they attacked.

My breath froze. So did my feet. I tried to move, but my legs were like Dad's over-cooked spaghetti noodles.

"You know it's haunted, right?" said a voice behind me.

Whirling around, I saw two older boys. They looked like twins. Their skin color was a little lighter than mine. One of them had dyed blond hair. The other had black dreadlocks.

The black-haired guy nodded. "The town says it's using the land for better Wi-Fi and cell signal. They're lying. They hope if they remodel the cemetery, the ghosts will leave." He stepped close. "You've noticed it, haven't you? Strange noises at night, kids disappearing into the mist, and your phone suddenly going dead?"

I swallowed hard. "I'm not allowed to have a phone."

"Because your parents don't want you to hear the ghosts cutting into your calls and wailing," said the blond kid.

The dark-haired one nodded at the graveyard. "That's where they meet up."

"You're trying to scare me. It's not working," I said, even though it was definitely working.

"Prove it," said the blond guy. "Go inside."

"No way," I said, trying not to shiver. "We're not allowed." I pointed at a large, white sign with red letters that said NO TRESPASSING.

"The construction workers won't be here for another hour. No one will know," said the boy with the dreads.

"Then you go," I said.

"What are you? Chicken?" asked the blond one.

"What are you?" I shot back. "Four years old? Calling me names won't work."

"Maybe this will." The blond kid grabbed my bag and launched it over the iron gates.

"Hey!" I yelled. "Bring it back!"

"Get it yourself," he said.

"We'll wait for you," said the black-haired guy.

I had to go inside. My parents would ground me if I lost the house key.

My heart crashed against my ribs as I reached the gate. Before I could do anything, it swung open, silently, as though it had been waiting for me.

The boys gasped.

"Well?" said the blond guy, his voice trembling. "Go on."

I took a deep breath and stepped inside.

2

Inside the cemetery, the fog was thick.

I wanted to run away, but I couldn't see the exit . . . or my bag. No way had the kid thrown it that far. Where was it?

I stepped on a bramble. It wriggled. I yelped, then tripped on another one. It squealed and cracked like a broken bone. I ran for where I thought the exit should be. Instead, I got lost.

The wind cried and swept the fog away. I was in the middle of the grave-yard. The trees in this section were dead.

No leaves. Their bark was split as though something big and menacing had sharpened its claws on their trunks.

Time to leave! I turned, and that's when I saw it—a living tree in the middle of all the dead ones.

It stood six feet tall, thick, with dark green leaves in the shape of tears. The soil around the tree was black and wet, but the grass was dead and brown. My breakfast rolled in my stomach as the smell of mold wafted my way. It seemed as though there was a face in the tree, staring at me. A prickle of unease skittered up my spine.

Everything in this area was dead . . . except the tree. It was strong and growing, almost as if it had fed off all the others. I took a cautious step backward. It was silly, but I didn't want to turn my back on the tree.

My ears pricked as a sound came behind me. "Who's there?" I called.

A twig snapped and I looked over my shoulder. I was alone. The wind blew and set the tree branches creaking. My chest tightened.

"Hello?" I raised my voice. The living tree's leaves rustled, tangling into each other, and formed the shape of a skull. A shiver ran through me.

I turned and ran.

Something reached out and grabbed me.

I seized the thing holding me.

"Ow!" yelled the thing. "What are you doing?"

I twisted free.

A girl with purple hair glared at me.

"Sorry." I let go of her hand.

She rubbed it. "What did you do that for?"

Telling her that I thought she was a ghost wasn't a good idea. "You scared me," I said. "Why didn't you answer me?"

She pulled an earbud out. "I didn't hear you."

"What are you doing here?" I asked.

"I saw my doofus older brothers in front of the gate," she said.

I blinked in surprise. Her brothers were big guys. Then again, she seemed fierce. I wouldn't mess with her.

She peered at me. "Did they dare you to come inside?"

I explained what had happened.

She sighed. "They're convinced the

cemetery is haunted," she said, "but they're too afraid to go in themselves. I ran them off." She peered at me again. "I thought I knew all the kids on the island."

"I'm new," I said. "I'm starting fourth grade."

She grinned. "That's cool! Me too! Not starting, I mean, I'm in fourth grade, too. I'll show you around and introduce you to everyone."

My chest loosened in relief. "That's awesome," I said. "Thanks!"

She held out her hand. "I'm Rokshar Kaya."

I took it. "Asim MacInroy."

"Your bag's back there." She jerked her thumb behind her.

Weird, I thought. *It wasn't there a*

minute ago. "Are your brothers right about the graveyard?" I asked as we headed to my bag. I dodged around the brambles, but Rokshar didn't seem to mind them.

She shrugged. "I want to be a scientist," she said, "and scientists are all about proving things."

"So, you think supernatural stuff is

just a bunch of stories?" I tried to keep disappointment out of my voice.

"If there was proof, I'd believe it," she said. "Do you believe?"

I did, but I didn't want to admit that, so I said, "Did you see that weird tree?"

She shook her head.

"The trees around it are dead," I said.

"So is the grass. The soil is black and wet, like oil. Come on, I'll show you." I needed Rokshar to tell me I was imagining things.

"Can't," she said, pointing at her smartwatch. "The bell's going to ring, and Mx. Hudson will make us miss recess if we're late."

"Miss—?" I asked.

"Mix," she corrected me. "*M-x*. Mx. Hudson is nonbinary."

"Got it," I said.

She led the way to the exit.

On the other side of the gates, we heard voices.

"It's the construction people," she whispered. "If they catch us, we'll be burned toast."

"Follow me," I whispered back. The workers had opened the gates. Keeping my eyes on them, I waved at Rokshar to run. Then I followed her out the exit. We sped away.

"That was awesome," I said.

"We make a great team!" She laughed as we walked to school. She turned to me with a gleam in her eye. "Tell me more about this weird tree."

3

"Earth to Asim, calling Asim MacInroy."

Just as I realized Mx. Hudson was talking to me, Rokshar poked me in the ribs.

"Ow!" I said, turning away from the window. "What did you do that for?"

She pointed at Mx. Hudson. "They're talking to you."

The teacher smiled at me. Their blue eyes crinkled. "Your answer?"

I blushed. I'd been thinking of the tree. "I didn't hear the question."

"What is the biome of Washington State?"

I blushed harder. "I don't know."

"It's a moist, temperate, coniferous forest," said Rokshar.

Mx. Hudson nodded. "Good job, Rokshar. Asim, I know the first day at a new school can be a lot to take in, but try to pay attention."

"I'm sorry," I said.

The teacher moved to the front of the class. "For our project, I'd like you to find a partner. We're going to do a joint assignment with the sixth graders— *Achoo!* We're go— *Achoo! Achoo! Achoo!*"

"Is it your allergies?" asked Rokshar.

Mx. Hudson nodded and grabbed the tissue box.

"You're allergic to everything," said a kid in the back row. "Maybe you're allergic to the assignment. To be safe, we shouldn't do it."

"Nice try, Max Rogers." Mx. Hudson laughed. "Rokshar," they said, "you're in charge for a minute. Max, please feed Duchess." They took their allergy pills and stepped outside the classroom.

"Let's be partners," Rokshar said to me.

"Deal!" I said. I watched Max take a

container of live mealworms and crickets. Then he scooped some into the dish for Duchess, the class's mascot. She was a yellow bearded dragon with green markings.

"Do you think Mx. Hudson gets us to feed Duchess because they're vegan?" Max asked Rokshar.

BUGS!

She frowned in confusion. "What do you mean?"

"Oh, like, because they'd feel weird feeding animals to Duchess?"

Rokshar shook her head. "A human's dietary needs and a reptile's needs are different. Mx. Hudson gets that." She grinned. "They get us to do it because they know we'll be good if that means a chance to hang with Duchess."

Our teacher returned. "Where were we? Oh, right. Grab a partner. We're going to pick some locations around Lion's Gate and collect samples of the town's biome. I'd like you and your partner to come up with a presentation for the class and teach us what you've learned."

An excited buzz went through the room. Anything to get us outside!

"We should collect samples around the playground," said one student.

"And by the town pool," said another.

Everyone shouted out their answers. Mine was going to the movie theater.

Rokshar raised her hand. "There's only one place we should go," she said. "The cemetery."

The class gasped. Then everyone went deadly quiet, waiting to see what Mx. Hudson would say.

4

"That's a great idea." They grinned. "The land's been unused for the last two years. It's the perfect place to explore."

"It's dangerous," I blurted. "There are overgrown roots." *Plus, a creepy ghost tree that's eating the other trees, with leaves that make the shape of a skull.*

"Everyone knows the cemetery is haunted," Max said.

Mx. Hudson's expression grew thoughtful. "We're going to go there," they said, "and not just for the assignment. The cemetery isn't haunted. Those spaces allow us to honor our families." They smiled at Max. "You'll see, there's nothing to be afraid of."

I hated it when adults said that about supernatural things. They were always wrong.

"You shouldn't have suggested the grave-yard," Max said to Rokshar as we stood in the coatroom after school.

"Why not?" Rokshar said. "It's a great place for the assignment."

Max scowled. "You're putting us all in danger!"

He stomped away.

"What did Max mean?" I asked Rokshar as we left school. "When he said you're putting us in danger?"

She kicked a pebble and it skipped down the road. "There's something wrong with this town," she said finally. "You're new, so you probably haven't noticed, but strange things happen here."

"Like voices coming across the water when no one's around," I said. "Laughter when I'm all alone."

"You've noticed it, too?" she said. She made a face. "Max and my brothers think it's supernatural stuff and we should stay away."

"What do you think?" I asked.

"The lab," she said. "They run secret projects. That's why we're the only town on the island and why we're surrounded by ocean and mountains. I bet the strange stuff is the experiments getting out of control, and the scientists trying to fix them. It makes sense." She stopped. "At least, it would make sense if I could find proof."

"The lab does experiments with plants, right?" I asked.

"Right," she said.

That might explain the weird tree. I hoped it did. Wonky science was less scary than a ghostly tree.

"I have a bunch of journals," she said. "I've been recording stuff. Want to come over and see?"

"Tomorrow?" I said. "I have to get permission."

She nodded. "Deal!"

I was a couple of blocks away from her

when I reached into my bag for my house key. Oh no! It was gone! There was only one place I could have lost it.

The cemetery.

My folks were going to be irritated if I lost the house key. This was the first time they'd ever trusted me to have one. I had to go back.

I jogged to the cemetery, hoping the construction people were around. They'd be mad, knowing I'd been in the graveyard this morning, but maybe they'd help me find the key.

"Rokshar's right." I tried to convince myself. "It's just a science experiment that's run wild." Totally. Except I was so scared, I heard my heartbeat in my ears.

I got to the main gates, but I didn't see anyone. My legs did their overcooked noodles impression, but I went inside.

It was even spookier than I remembered. I tried to retrace my steps to where I'd lost my bag.

But each path looked the same as all the others. Soon, I was lost, and I found myself by the grove of dead trees. I crept forward, but I couldn't believe what I saw.

The ghost tree from this morning had grown. Now it was almost fourteen feet tall, with a thick trunk. The pool of black ink surrounding it was bigger, too. It slid along the dead grass and left burned

patches. The worst part was the dead trees around it.

This morning, they'd been leafless and cracked. Now they were bowed and bent. Their trunks looked like something had squeezed them. I heard moaning, as though they were in pain.

Stop it! I thought. *The moaning is probably the hum from the cables the construction team is putting in.*

Then I noticed an object shining on the cobblestones. My key. How did it end up so far from my bag?

The leaves of the ghost tree rustled, and it sounded as though it was laughing, daring me to come closer.

I pushed down my fear. *Don't be a coward!* I told myself. *It's just a tree!* As I moved toward it, I heard footsteps coming up the path, fast, heading straight for me.

I ducked behind a clump of bushes, then
peeked out. It was a construction worker.
"As soon as dinner's finished," he spoke
into his cell, "we can play that video
game—*Princess Zombie Warriors*." He lis-
tened to the person on the other end, then
laughed. "I love you, too, Max." He hung
up the phone, then noticed the tree. "I
don't remember you," he said. He frowned
as he saw the black pool. The man bent
down and reached out his hand.

Before I could yell, *Don't touch it!* the man stuck his hand in the goo. He yelped and pulled back, waving his fingers as though they'd been burned. The man blew on his skin and stared at the tree.

"Nelson, there you are." A short man ran up to him. "I've been looking for you. We need your help—"

"You always need my help," Nelson barked. "Can't you do anything by yourself?"

His coworker stepped back. "You said we're free to ask for help," he said quietly.

"Why are you so useless?" Nelson growled, and stomped away.

The man watched him for a moment with a puzzled look on his face. He shuffled after him.

I came out from the bushes. Then I

turned back to the ghost tree. Its branches shivered and formed a face with a menacing smile.

I grabbed my key and ran out of the cemetery.

"Anything exciting happen today?" Mom asked as I helped with dinner.

I wanted to tell her about the tree. If I did that, though, I'd have to tell her about sneaking into a restricted area. "I made a friend." I thought about Rokshar and her journals. "She's going to help me learn about the town."

"Lucky!" she said. "I would love to have someone show me around. Especially the *spooky* parts." Her grin faded to a stern look. "You two aren't going anywhere unsafe, right?"

Now I was really glad I hadn't told her about going into the cemetery! "Of course not!" I tried to sound casual and asked, "Have you heard of any stories with ghost trees?"

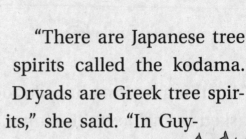

Kodama

Dryads

Dutchman tree

"There are Japanese tree spirits called the kodama. Dryads are Greek tree spirits," she said. "In Guyana, there are the Dutchman trees. They're silk cotton trees. Some say the souls of enslaved people live in them, but I was always told it was the Dutch slave owners who were trapped. Anyone who tries to cut down the tree or comes too close will be injured, or worse."

My body shook. The way the tree had destroyed all the nature around it, how it turned the construction guy mean, and how it had destroyed everything in its path—it must be a Dutchman tree with the ghost of a slave owner in it.

"Why are you asking?" Mom said.

I racked my brain for a good reason. "We're studying biomes, and I saw a creepy tree. I got curious," I said as Dad came inside. "Your story sounds scary. Having to live with ghost trees."

"Hmm." Mom looked at me like she knew I was holding back, but she didn't push. "My mom always said you can destroy them with salt."

She seemed as though she was going to ask some tough questions, so I said, "After dinner, I'll add those stories to our notebooks."

"That's a great idea." Mom's voice jumped with excitement. "I'll illustrate them when you're done."

Even though I'd suggested adding the

stories to the notebooks to distract her from my questions, I got excited, too. Mom was great at drawing, and I couldn't wait to expand our homemade encyclopedia and grow our list of supernatural creatures.

Dad set the table, and I put our bowls of cauliflower and pea soup on the table.

"Finally!" I sat down. "I'm starving."

"Nice to meet you, Starving," said Dad. "I'm Dad."

I groaned.

My parents laughed.

While we were eating, I asked, "What kinds of things do people do at Eden Lab?"

Mom and Dad hesitated.

"I can tell you that some teams look for medicines," Dad said. "Others are building new technology. A few work with plants, and some folks study the weather."

"The lab works with plants?" I said. "Like making trees grow fast?"

Dad swallowed his soup and thought. "How fast?"

"Like, eight feet in a few hours?" I asked.

Dad laughed. "That's impossible!"

"But you said some of the teams work on plants," I said. "Maybe they've come up

HA HA HA HA

with a new supergrowth formula. Maybe it got into town."

Dad grew serious. "Kiddo, the lab is very strict about its experiments," he said. "We have safeguards to protect the town." Dad squeezed my hand. "There's nothing to be afraid of with the lab, especially not a supergrowth formula."

Great. Except every time an adult told me not to be afraid, that was exactly what I felt.

6

"Ugh," said Rokshar when I saw her at school the next morning. "Why did you talk to your parents? They work for a top secret lab; they can't tell you the truth. I gave up asking my parents about the lab a long time ago."

The idea that my parents would keep secrets stung. "Maybe, but they wouldn't lie to me."

"They might not be able to tell you everything. It's an adult thing." Rokshar dug into her bag and pulled out an apple tart. She broke it in half and handed me a piece.

As we ate, I told her about Nelson and the tree.

"Are you sure it grew that quickly?" she asked. "Maybe you saw another tree?"

I shook my head. "No, it was the same tree. Dad says no tree can grow that fast."

"But he doesn't work with plants," she pointed out. "He might not know."

"Maybe," I agreed. "But Nelson's personality changed as soon as he touched that black oil. Plus, it burned his hand. I wish you'd been there to see."

She dug back into her bag. "We can't always be together. That's why I got us these." She pulled out two journals.

I took the purple one, and she kept the blue.

"We can record our observations," she

said. "Then we can compare and share information. I'm using the scientific method to study the weird things," she said.

"I'll use it, too," I said. "That way, we're the same." I took out my pencil and started to write. Step One, my question.

The tree in the middle of the graveyard seems to be eating the other trees and growing very fast. It's surrounded by black liquid that burns skin and turns people mean.

I tapped the pencil against my chin.

It also makes creepy faces. What is causing this?

Step Two, my hypothesis.

The tree is inhabited by a ghost that doesn't like people.

Step Three, my evidence, research, and observations.

- The tree grew eight feet in eight hours.
- The liquid burned Nelson's hand.
- Nelson went from cheerful to grumpy after he touched the liquid.

Rokshar looked over my shoulder. "That's good," she said, "but everything can be explained scientifically. The sap of some trees makes your skin blister. If I'd just burned my hand, like Nelson, I'd be grumpy, too." She tilted her head. "Certain kinds of bamboo can grow three feet in a day. I don't know how the tree grew so fast, but I bet it's plant food."

She made good points, but I couldn't shake the feeling that she was wrong and I was right.

My class waited for the sixth graders and chaperones in front of the cemetery gates. Rokshar and I went up to Mx. Hudson. I asked, "Have you ever heard of a tree that grew eight feet in a day?"

Their eyes went wide. "In a day? No, hybrid poplars can add five feet, but that's in a year."

I wanted to ask more, but the other groups arrived. I saw Rokshar's brothers with the sixth-grade class.

"The blond one's Devlin," she said as they walked up to us. "The dark-haired one is Malachi."

"Hey, Rock Star," said Malachi.

Devlin looked at me. "Hey, do I know you?"

I stared at him. "Are you kidding? You threw my bag over the cemetery wall!"

He shrugged. "We do that to a lot of kids. How else will we prove the grave-yard is haunted? What's your name, anyway?"

"Asim," I said.

"Ha! Rock Star and Awesome," he said. "Cool!"

I rolled my eyes as we gathered in front of the teachers.

Max came up to us. "If I get carried off by a ghost," he said to Rokshar, "I'm coming back and haunting you!"

Mx. Hudson called for quiet. "This is Nelson, the construction foreperson," they said. "Please follow his rules."

"This isn't a playground," barked Nelson. "No horsing around, no touching anything!"

Mx. Hudson cleared their throat. "Er, we'll be collecting samples of the plants for our project. We'll need to touch things."

"Fine," he growled, "but be careful around the sewer lines or else—BOOM!"

We jumped back.

Max tapped Nelson's arm as he stomped away.

Nelson grabbed Max's coat. "What do you want?"

"Uncle Nelson, it's me," Max stammered. "Are you still coming to dinner? We're going to play *Princess Zombie Warriors.*"

"I don't have time for your nonsense!"

Nelson shouted. He shoved Max aside and rushed off.

"That was unreal," said Max, his eyes wide. "Uncle Nelson is usually the happiest, nicest guy." He rubbed his arm. "He'd never push me!"

Malachi held his nose. "But did he shower? Yuck."

He smells like the tree, I thought, *like rotting garbage.*

Mx. Hudson led us into the cemetery.

"Come with me," I said to Rokshar, Devlin, Malachi, and Max. "I want you to see this tree." I glanced at Rokshar. "I think it might have a ghost in it."

This time, I didn't get lost. But I wished I had. When we got to it, Devlin's mouth dropped open. Malachi hung back, and Max hid behind Rokshar.

"I told you this place was haunted!"

cried Max. "Let's go! I don't care if I fail this assignment!"

The trees here had been destroyed.

There were piles of broken trunks and shredded branches.

"Did someone blow up the trees?" wondered Malachi. "There's nothing left here but toothpicks!"

"That's not the worst of it," I said. I wiped my clammy palms on my jeans and pointed. "Look."

7

The ghost tree was now eighteen feet tall. There were cracks in the ground as if it had been struck by lightning. The black oil was still there. The tree was black now, too. Large thorns grew from its twisted trunk. Its leaves were blood red and ended in sharp points.

"That can't be your tree," breathed Rokshar. "Nothing can grow that fast."

"It looks evil," said Devlin. He pointed at the three holes in the trunk. "Look! It has a face."

He was right. There were two eyes and a gaping mouth.

It's hungry, I thought. *It's eaten all the trees. Now it wants more.*

The tree's eyes seemed to look at me.

I gulped. *It wants* us.

"We should take a sample," said Rokshar.

She stepped toward the tree, but I pulled her back. "It's not safe," I said.

"He's right," said Malachi, sniffing the air. "It smells like Max's uncle." His nose wrinkled. "Gross."

I told them about seeing Nelson touch the liquid.

Everyone but Rokshar stepped back. "If this tree is haunted by a ghost," she said, "we need to prove it. But if something is

leaking from the lab and poisoning the ground, we need proof of that, too." She reached into her bag and pulled out a container and a spoon.

Rokshar marched up to the liquid. She hesitated.

"She's not going to do it," said Max.

"You don't know our sister," said Malachi.

She glanced back at us. Rokshar's shoulders straightened. She crouched by the oil. Her nose wrinkled at the smell.

"We need to help her," I said.

"I'm not going over there," said Max.

The others nodded in agreement.

I jogged over to Rokshar. "I'll hold the container."

She smiled with relief. "Thanks." Rokshar dipped her spoon into the goo.

The oil hissed and fizzed, and smoke spiraled upward.

We yelped and scrambled back. She pulled out the spoon.

We stared at the smoking remains.

"Run!" yelled Devlin. "Before the tree eats you!"

We ran back to the group.

"I have the

spoon," Rokshar panted. "I'll use my science kit at home to test what's left of it."

"You can't bring it into the house," cried Malachi. "The goo will eat all of us!"

"What's going to eat you?" Mx. Hudson came up beside us.

"That tree," said Max. "It's got an evil face, and it eats metal!"

Rokshar held up the spoon for Mx. Hudson to see.

"Let me get you a sample," they said.

"No!" I yelled, but they were already walking to the tree.

We watched in horror as our teacher got close to the bark. Just as they looked up, the leaves of the tree shivered. Thick red sap rained down.

Mx. Hudson began to scream.

8

"Is Mx. Hudson going to be okay?" I watched one of the parents help them into a car and drive away with them.

"It was an allergic reaction," said a chaperone. "They'll be fine."

"That tree wants to eat everyone," said Malachi as we walked back to school. "That wasn't an allergy attack."

"It could have been," said Rokshar. "There are certain nuts that can strip the enamel off your teeth."

Devlin looked at me. "You know it's a ghost, right?"

I nodded.

Devlin took paper and a pencil out of his bag. "Everyone write down their emails and phone numbers," he said. "We have to save the town from the tree."

Max went first. "I'll do anything to help my uncle. Mx. Hudson, too. They're the nicest teacher in the whole school!"

I went next.

Malachi took the pencil and paper from me. He started to write.

Devlin snatched it away. "I already have your information, goof!"

When we got to our classroom, Principal Chin took us to the library. I searched for stories on tree ghosts. Rokshar searched for a scientific explanation for the tree's toxicity. Max looked for ways to stop ghosts.

"What did you find?" I asked when the lunch bell rang.

"An extra egg in a cake mix makes it fluffy," said Max.

Rokshar and I stared at him.

"What?" He rubbed his stomach. "I get hungry when I'm worried. I got lost in the cookbook section. Sorry," he said glumly.

"That's okay," I said. "I know salt repels ghosts."

Max plucked at a loose thread on his T-shirt. "Does that mean we throw salt on my uncle?"

"That's only if he's possessed by a ghost," Rokshar said as we walked to the cafeteria. "We still don't know if anything supernatural is going on. Your uncle might just be grumpy from the burn on his hand. As for the tree, one of the library books said it could be a fungus infection."

"Look! There's Mx. Hudson," Max said. Our teacher went into the classroom.

"Come on," said Rokshar. "If it was an allergic reaction, Mx. Hudson will tell us."

"And if it's a ghost?" I asked.

She straightened her shoulders. "We'll save the town."

Rokshar ran to the classroom, then slammed to a stop. I crashed into her back. Max headbutted my shoulder.

"Ow!" he said. "What—"

I slapped my hand over his mouth as he pointed.

Our teacher hovered over Duchess's habitat. Mx. Hudson had the container of bugs and was greedily devouring them.

We escaped down the hall.

"That was weird," said Max.

"Maybe the allergy shot is giving them strange cravings," Rokshar said, her face worried.

"Mx. Hudson is vegan," Max said. "No way would they eat bugs!"

"The tree is hurting people," I said. "We have to stop it."

After dinner, I logged on to my computer. There was a message from Malachi.

> Mx. Hudson and Max's uncle Nelson must be saved! Hurry up and find the answers!

"Make us do the work," I muttered. I went online and researched what Mom had said about salt. I made some notes in my journal.

> Salt is good at stopping ghosts, but pink salt is better.

I added the line that made me tremble.

> It must be applied to the vessel housing the ghost.

A message from Max made me look up.

Horrible news!!! My uncle came over and he was terrible!! He smells SO BAD!! He yelled at my mom, and he ate everything. EVERYTHING! He even took food from other people's plates! And he scared Toby, my dog. He never does that! Uncle Nelson and Toby love each other!!!! I saw him eating chicken bones from the garbage, too! GROSS!! WE NEED TO STOP THIS GHOST TREE!

I logged off. Max was right, and I knew how we could start.

"That tree's infected two people," said Devlin as we headed to school. "We have to destroy it before it infects the whole town."

"Did you get any answers from your science kit?" I asked Rokshar.

Malachi rolled his eyes. "Yeah, she found out that black oily stuff is flammable."

"I used litmus paper to see if the

substance was an acid or a base," said Rokshar. "It set the paper on fire."

"That's because it was ghost goo," said Devlin.

"There's no proof," she said.

"There might be a way to get proof," I said. "Ghosts hate salt. If there's one inhabiting the tree or Nelson and Mx. Hudson, they'll have a bad reaction to salt."

"How?" asked Rokshar. "Slugs don't like salt, either."

"But humans need salt to survive," I said. "If Mx. Hudson is repelled by the salt, then we'll have part of our answer."

Malachi frowned. "How are you going to do it?"

I said, "I have a plan."

Max, Rokshar, and I went to class. Our teacher was there.

They looked horrible. Their hair was oily and limp. There were dark smudges under their eyes, and their fingernails were yellow.

"Are you okay?" I asked them.

"I'm fine," Mx. Hudson snarled. They pulled out a bag of beef jerky from their drawer and tore into it.

Max's eyes widened.

Rokshar glanced at me. "Time for your test," she whispered.

"What are you going to do?" asked Max.

"You said your uncle ate everything. He even took other people's food." I pulled out a container. "If there's a ghost in Mx. Hudson and your uncle, that's probably why they're eating so much."

"Be careful," said Max.

"Don't worry," I told him. My words were brave, but I wasn't. My legs were doing their overcooked noodle thing, and my throat was so tight I could barely breathe. As I got closer to my teacher, my eyes watered at the sour smell coming off them. "Mx. Hudson, if you're still hungry, I have—"

They snatched the container out of my grasp. Mx. Hudson ripped off the top and dug their hand in it. They howled and flung the container away. Salt spilled to the ground. Mx. Hudson's hand was red and blistering. They stared at me with glowing eyes.

The ghost realizes I know how to stop it, I thought.

Mx. Hudson clutched their arm and stormed out of the room.

I swept the salt into the garbage. "Touching salt hurts them." I looked over at Rokshar. "That's proof."

"But Mx. Hudson's allergic to everything," she said.

Max looked miserable. "It's true. The salt didn't save them."

"Because we need more of it," I said. I remembered my research. "We need pink salt. Would the grocery store have that?"

"I don't have money," Max said morosely. "Do you?"

"I can make a solution if you bring salt," said Rokshar. "Pink salt is regular salt, but it has calcium, potassium, magnesium, and iron in it."

"Trust me," I said. "The salt will work."

"Come to my house tonight and bring as much as you can," said Rokshar.

"Bring as much of what as you can?"

We jumped at Mx. Hudson's voice. I whirled around. They stood behind us.

Their eyes narrowed into slits. "What are you mixing up?"

"For the biome assignment," said Rokshar. "Washington State is one of the largest producers of apples and raspberries. We're going to make a crumble for the class." She rushed her words.

"Don't worry, we'll make sure it's vegan for you," said Max. He slapped his hand over his mouth.

Mx. Hudson's eyes slid to their desk, where the beef jerky sat. Their gaze turned to us. "Yes," they said. "Vegan."

10

We met in Rokshar's room, and I told everyone my plan.

"We're all going to die!" Max wailed. "You want us to throw salt on the tree's roots? It's going to eat us!"

"Stop yelling!" Devlin said. "Our parents will hear you!"

"If we destroy the tree, we destroy the ghost," I said. "It'll save the town."

"We have to do it," said Malachi.

Rokshar yelled, "Mom, Dad, we're going on a nature walk!"

"Have fun!" Mrs. Kaya called up. "Don't be home too late!"

"Come on," I said grimly. "Let's go before it gets dark." *Or before I lose my nerve.*

We stood at the cemetery gates.

"Maybe we can make a catapult and launch the salt at the tree," Malachi said shakily. "Then we don't have to go into the graveyard."

"No," I said, shaking my head. "We have to get the salt on the roots. Kill the roots, kill the tree."

"Go ahead, Rokshar," said Devlin. "We're right behind you."

She rolled her eyes. "Yeah, ten feet behind."

I moved to the gate, but it swung open on its own.

"This is bad," moaned Max. "It knows we're coming."

"We have to do this for your uncle and Mx. Hudson," I said.

He brightened. "I brought some stuff to help us."

"We did too," said Devlin, patting his backpack.

Max opened his bag. Inside were cartons of milk and bags of pumpkin seeds, figs, and almonds, along with a big container of pasta.

We stared.

"Snacks," he said proudly.

"How does this help?" Malachi asked.

"Keeping your energy up keeps you in fighting shape," huffed Max.

"This was good thinking," I told him, and helped him put everything back in his bag.

"Let's go before it's too late," said Rokshar.

Evil laughter echoed around us.

"It's already too late," said voices from the shadows.

Nelson and Mx. Hudson stepped out from the darkness.

"Run!" I yelled. "Get to the tree!"

We raced through the graveyard, leaping over roots.

Nelson and Mx. Hudson chased us.

Mx. Hudson was on my heels. They grabbed my collar. I shuddered at their

cold, slimy hands. Mx. Hudson yanked
me backward. I pulled free of my jacket.
Malachi and Devlin tackled them.

Max stumbled.

"Keep going!" I grasped his arm and
pulled him along.

Nelson raced for Rokshar.

Max and I charged after him. I got in
front of Nelson. Max pushed his uncle,

and I ducked in front of him. Nelson tripped and slammed to the ground. I jumped over him and kept running.

The brambles and roots began to wriggle. They rose from the ground and reached for us. One of them snapped upright, like a cobra, and snatched Rokshar. It held her aloft as another one began to wind around her body.

Max and I ran to the roots and pulled. I gagged. They smelled like rotting meat.

We fought, but the roots outnumbered us. They twisted around my body and squeezed tight. My ribs hurt, and my lungs burned. There were sparks of light in my eyes.

Then, suddenly, I was free! I gasped for air.

I blinked and focused. Malachi and Devlin were spraying something at the roots.

"Weed killer!" said Devlin. He sprayed a root. It squealed and recoiled from the liquid. He sprayed the roots that held Max. They shrieked and let go of him.

"Get away from my sister!" Malachi yelled, spraying the brambles.

Screaming, they dropped her.

"We have to keep going!" Rokshar panted.

"Not so fast!" Mx. Hudson appeared

from the shadows, with Nelson beside them.

Nelson laughed at the bottles. "I'm not afraid of weed killer!"

My friends and I glanced at each other. Then we threw the bottles at the two of them. They ducked out of the way.

We ran for the tree.

A heavy weight smashed into my shoulder. I crashed to the ground.

"Give up," Mx. Hudson breathed.

I choked at their smelly breath.

Devlin jumped on the teacher and wrestled them off me.

Malachi grabbed Nelson and shoved him to the ground.

Rokshar, Max, and I raced for the tree. My lungs burned, but I kept going. When we got close, the ground shook and rumbled. The tree's roots burst from the earth and tried to wrap around our feet. We zigged and zagged. Rokshar sped up, panting hard, and flung a bag of salt at the tree. I flung another bag. So did Max.

The tree screamed as the salt hit its roots. Pink, red, and orange light exploded all around it. The roots thrashed and writhed.

One of them caught my face. The pain seared my skin.

"It's not enough!" cried Max.

The tree shuddered, but it wouldn't die.

Rokshar pulled Max's bag off his shoulders. She launched it at the base of the tree. It convulsed. A terrifying groan vibrated the ground.

"Run!" I screamed.

The three of us raced back to Devlin and Malachi. Nelson and Mx. Hudson

lay on the ground. Rokshar's brothers dragged the adults to their feet.

We raced for the exit just as the tree exploded.

11

By the time we got to the gates, the emergency crews were there. The paramedics checked us out, and the officers called our parents.

"You're a hero," I said to Max.

"Don't tease me," he said. "I've had a hard night!"

"I'm not," I said. "If it hadn't been for your snacks, that tree would still be alive. Remember what Rokshar said about pink salt? It was different from regular salt because it had more calcium, iron, and magnesium. Milk has tons of calcium, and your snacks had loads of iron."

"Wow," he said. "Who knew food had that kind of power?"

Devlin tapped Rokshar. "Do you believe us now? That graveyard had a ghost."

"I agree very weird things happened," she said, "but we still don't have proof."

Malachi sighed. "The tree tried to kill you, remember?"

"To prove something is true," she said, "scientists have to be able to repeat the experiment."

Malachi looked at her in disbelief. "Are you saying you want that ghost tree back?"

"No!" she said. "There's just no way to prove the ghost existed." She nudged her brothers. "I saw evidence you're braver than I thought, though."

"Aww. . . ." Devlin blushed.

"You're our sister, and these are your friends," said Malachi. "We couldn't let anything happen to you guys."

"Max?" Nelson said from his stretcher. "What am I doing here?"

Max scrambled to his uncle's side.

The rest of us checked on Mx. Hudson.

"What a terrible allergic reaction," they said. "I don't remember anything after touching the tree. The doctors said Nelson and I are lucky you were around to save us from the sewer explosion."

The paramedics wheeled them into the ambulance as our parents arrived.

"Don't tell anyone what really happened," said Malachi. "They'll never believe us!"

"The police say you and your friends are heroes," Dad said as we walked home. "They say a sewer line exploded, and if you hadn't been there to pull Nelson and Mx. Hudson to safety, they would have been seriously hurt."

Mom peered at me. "Funny how you all happened to be at the cemetery at the right time." She peered harder. "And funny how all the salt is gone from the kitchen."

"It was for the biome assignment," I said.

"You're not going to be chasing down any other strange things in town, are you?" she asked, giving me a firm look.

I glanced up as an object flew over-head. It hovered over us, then disappeared in a trail of green light. "The assignment is done," I said. "We won't be looking at trees for a while."

"We don't want you chasing trouble," said Dad. "Asim, I'm serious!"

"Nice to meet you, Serious," I said. "My name is Asim."

Dad and Mom groaned.

I laughed.

Notes from Rokshar's Journal

- Many of the phenomena my friends and I experienced can be explained scientifically.

- Mx. Hudson's reaction to the tree: My teacher is allergic to everything. They might have had a reaction to the sap and/or pollen of the tree. For example, all parts of the manchineel tree are toxic to humans. Maybe the tree in the cemetery was a manchineel hybrid.

- The face in the tree: There is a tendency for human beings to see faces in objects like clouds, cars, and houses. This is known as pareidolia.

- However, there are things I can't explain scientifically. What caused the tree to grow so fast? Why did Mx. Hudson and

Max's uncle smell like the tree? What was the cause of their sudden personality changes? And why did they immediately return to their old selves once the tree was destroyed?

- Is it possible that adding the minerals to regular salt acted as an antifungal agent? I will conduct experiments to find out.

- I'm left with no proof, for either a supernatural or a scientific cause.

- Conclusion: I cannot say whether the tree in the graveyard was a Dutchman tree.

Notes from Asim's Journal

* I'm positive that we faced down the ghost of a slave owner, and I have proof.

* The tree's growth was impossible under natural circumstances.

* The tree had a face, and its expressions seemed to change in reaction to our conversations.

* Both adults' personalities

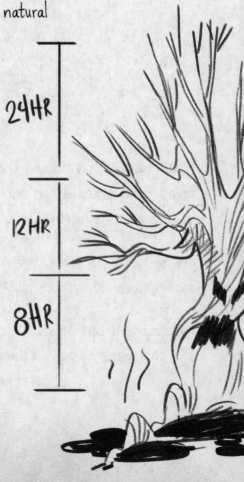

Buy salt!

changed after they touched the tree. They became violent, greedy, and cruel. Once the tree was destroyed, both Mx. Hudson and Nelson became nice again.

* Salt, a ghost repellent, destroyed the tree.

* Conclusion: My friends and I saved two adults—maybe the entire town—from a ghostly possession.

Smelly

weird oil

Scary Roots

Author's Note

The tree that inspired this story is known by many names in Guyana. It has been called the Jumbie tree, the Tree in the Middle of the Road, and the Dutchman tree. The species of tree is the silk cotton tree, and many believe it has mystical roots and great supernatural powers.

There are tales of Dutch enslavers who would bury their gold under the tree, then kill an enslaved person because they believed that person's spirit would guard the gold.

The stories I was told as a child are different. My grandmother would tell me to beware the Dutchman tree and stay away from it. The tree, she said, held the spirits of Dutch slave owners as punishment for their actions in life. Those ghosts would harm anyone who came too close.

But if you asked my grandfather, it was the Jumbie tree. It was home to spirits that would sit under it late at night. The ghosts didn't like to be disturbed, especially at night, and I was warned to never get close.

Then there is the account of the Tree in the Middle of the Road, a tree in Mahaicony, Guyana. Anyone who tries to destroy it will meet a terrible fate. There have been disappearances and deaths blamed on the tree. So much so that former President Bharrat Jagdeo decreed that the tree is to be left alone, and no one is allowed to cut it down.

Nobody knows how the ghosts get into the trees or why they are trapped by them, but we all know it's best to stay away from them!

GET A SNEAK PEEK AT THE NEXT BOOK IN THE SPOOKY SLEUTHS SERIES.

Turn the page . . . if you dare!

When we got to school, Mx. Hudson was feeding Duchess. "Change of plans for today," they said. "Our Wi-Fi is down. Someone vandalized the cables in the cemetery and around town."

"That's terrible!" I said, pretending to be surprised. "Why would anyone do that?"

Mx. Hudson sighed. "Some people like the remoteness of our town. Look at Mr. Maan. He travels a lot, but when he comes back, all he wants to do is spend time in the forest."

Just then, Mr. Maan came into the room. "The principal told me about the vandalism," he said, trying to hide his smile. "How horrible."

I have to add him being happy about the vandalism to my journal, I thought.

He brushed his sleeve and dirt fell.

Dirt? Like from being in the cemetery? I wondered.

Mr. Maan walked away, and I stared at him. Yesterday, he'd been tall and pale. Today, he seemed taller, brighter . . . just like the light in the cemetery. I leaned toward my friends. "Is he glowing?" I whispered.

"It's his white clothing," Rokshar whispered back. "It's reflecting the light."

She was the smartest person I knew. Maybe she was right about Mr. Maan. Maybe he was grouchy because of the noise. And maybe his suit was reflecting the classroom lights. Or maybe he was a supernatural creature, and he was gaining power because the full moon was near. I raised my hand and said, "Mr. Maan, you seemed unhappy when we talked about traveling to the moon—"

"I don't blame him," said Mx. Hudson as they put a photo of the moon on the whiteboard. "Until we learn how to care for Earth, we shouldn't be leaving it."

I looked at Mr. Maan to see if he agreed, but he wasn't listening. He was staring at the photo. His body seemed to go fuzzy and soft. Mr. Maan's eyes turned white and began to shimmer.

I froze. Before I could nudge Rokshar or Max, I blinked, and he returned to normal. Had I imagined it, or had Mr. Maan transformed when he looked at the moon?

"He might have an eye condition that makes it seem like his eyes go white in certain light," said Rokshar.

It was after school. Rokshar had invited Max and me over for dinner. We were eating cookies for dessert in her kitchen and talking about what I had seen.

"Have you heard of anything like that?" asked Devlin.

"No," she admitted, "but there's lots I don't know."

Malachi poked her. "You know everything."

She grinned and nudged him back.

"It's not an eye condition," I said. "It's proof that Mr. Maan is a supernatural creature. His body definitely got blurry. And he glows, just like the light at the cemetery. I bet he's the giant—I bet he can make himself taller or shorter if he wants."

"How do we get evidence that Mr. Maan isn't human?" asked Malachi.

"In some TV shows," I said, "the alien's blood is a different color. Maybe supernatural creatures are similar."

Rokshar shook her head. "Humans can have blood conditions that make their skin look blue."

"My granddad has diabetes, and one time, it made his breath smell really sweet," said Max. "Would something like that be proof?"

"Do you want to get close to Mr. Maan and smell his breath?" asked Malachi.

Max shuddered. "No."

"Sweat," I said. "Maybe there's something in his sweat."

"Seriously," Devlin groaned. "Stop."

Rokshar thought about it. "We need to go to the forest this weekend and look for clues."

After school on Wednesday, I walked home alone. I stopped, pulled out my journal, and added in what I'd learned.

* There was a light in the cemetery, and someone ripped up the Wi-Fi cables. Mr. Maan was happy about this.

* Some people (like Mr. Maan) want Lion's Gate to stay remote.

* Was he the light we saw at the cemetery?

I closed my book. Mr. Maan had turned gooey when he saw the moon. I put that together with Dad's talk about light pollution. Could it be that Mr. Maan was here because Lion's Gate had the best view of the moon?

No, that didn't make sense. The moon could be seen from any place on Earth. Still . . . I couldn't shake the feeling Mr. Maan, the moon, the light, and the vandalism were connected.